Black Lagoon® Adventures

SPECIAL EDITION #3:

HUBIE COOL: SUPERHERO

Black Lagoon® Adventures
SPECIAL EDITION #3:

HUBIE COOL: SUPERHERO

CRACK!

FLASH!

by Mike Thaler
Illustrated by Jared Lee

SCHOLASTIC INC.

For Patty, my super hero wife!
—M.T.

to Jaden Blair
—J.L.

INVISIBLE
MOUSE

Text copyright © 2017 by Mike Thaler
Illustrations copyright © 2017 by Jared Lee

ISBN 978-1-338-17220-1

10 9 8 7 6 5 4 3 2 1   17 18 19 20 21

Printed in the U.S.A.   40
First printing 2017

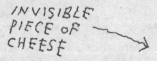

INVISIBLE
PIECE OF
CHEESE

EGGS
↓

CONTENTS

CHAPTER 1
MY WORD

Every superhero has a magic word that gives them their superpowers.

One says, "Shazam!"

One says, "Up, up and away!"

I say, "Bummer!"

And in a flash I become Earthman, defender of the environment, guardian of the ozone, and enemy of litter.

EARTH →

MOON

EARTHMAN

STANDING FIRM IN HIS QUEST

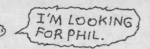

By day, I am an almost normal third-grade student—doing my homework, reading comic books, and talking to my dog.

But at the first sign of trouble I say, "Bummer!"

There's a flash of lightning, a clap of thunder, a drum roll, and ta-da!

Earthman appears in yellow pajamas and a yellow cape, ready to pummel polluters and trample trashers!

I'm titanic!

I'm organic!

I'm Earthman!

THE TITANIC →

8

CHAPTER 2
CLEAN OUT OF HIS MIND

My archenemy is the evil weevil Trashman and his army of litterbug polluters.

They come from the planet Polluto, a toxic waste site in space, and are constantly searching the universe for anything green.

For *green* means clean and it bugs them.

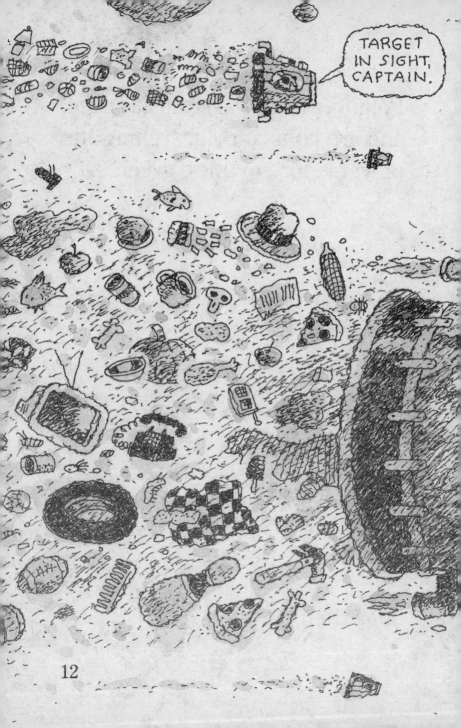

They travel across the galaxy in their giant stinky garbage can rocket ships leaving trails of smog, trash, and waste on their way to an unsuspecting planet.

CHAPTER 3
DOWN IN THE DUMPS

Earthman comes from the planet Vegan. A planet that was totally clean. There was a trash can on every corner and people used them.

I'M SO HAPPY.

The air was pure and the sky was blue. There were trees and flowers everywhere. All the water was clean and clear.

Then one day the planet was invaded by Trashman and his rabble of rubble.

They attacked the air and polluted the water. They cut down all the trees and trampled all the flowers. The planet Vegan was turned from a pure paradise into a toxic dump.

My mom, in an effort to save us, took me and my dog in a solar-powered rocket and traveled to Earth.

17

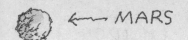
← MARS

"Hubie, where on earth are you?"

"Right here, Mom."

"Are you ready for dinner?"

"Yes, Mom."

"Did you wash your hands?"

"Twice!"

"Good boy."

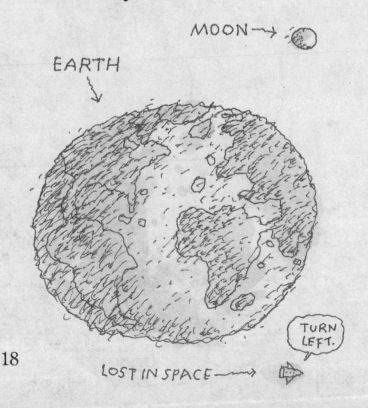

MOON →

EARTH

TURN LEFT.

LOST IN SPACE →

19

CHAPTER 4
IN SINK

"It's time for bed, Hubie. Did you brush your teeth?"

"I sure did, and I didn't keep the water running. I only used what I needed."

"Good boy."

OCTOPUS
↓

BONE
↓

20

21

"Mom, will you read to me about how there are giant islands of plastic trash bags filling up the ocean?"

"Wouldn't you rather hear a fairy tale?"

"No, I'd rather hear about the great Pacific garbage patch."

"Oh, Hubie, it will give you nightmares."

"Mom, it *is* a nightmare!"

BAT

← BAT

CHAPTER 5
A RECYCLOPSE

CAPTAIN, I NEED TO SPEAK TO YOU.

That night I did have a nightmare. I dreamed I was in a submarine under the ocean. Something was seriously wrong and we were slowly running out of oxygen.

I'M VERY HUNGRY.

OH GREAT.

25

When we tried to reach the surface we couldn't because the top of the sea had turned to plastic. I woke up, pushed back my covers, and took a deep breath. It was just a bad dream— or was it?

NOT A SEAHORSE

CHAPTER 6
WASTE-LAND

SIT UP, SPOT.

The next day at lunchtime there were other problems.

"Eric, are you going to eat everything on your tray?"

"Not the spoon and the fork," sneered Eric.

"What about the food?"

"I don't know."

"You took three hamburgers and a mountain of French fries."

"I was hungry, but you just ruined my appetite," snarled Eric.

"You know, it's wrong to waste food," I proclaim.

"Well, you're wasting your breath. I'll eat it if I want to!"

"Your eyes are bigger than your stomach."

"Well, your mouth is bigger than your brain."

"Well, your feet are bigger than your nose."

"Well . . ."

"Now, boys, lunchtime is over. It's time for recess," said Wanda Belch.

Eric dumped his tray into a garbage can and we went out to play.

CHAPTER 7
IF NOT ME, WHO?

"Hubie, what are you doing?" asked Eric.

"I'm picking up this gum wrapper."

"Why? It's not yours."

"Yes, Eric, but it's our planet."

"Are you going to save the world?"

"Saving the world starts with you and me," I said.

GUM→ ▭

FERRARI ⟶

"Well, if it's my world I want a million dollars and a Ferrari!"

"Eric, it's our world to take care of."

"Well, I'm not working for nothing!"

33

"Eric, the world takes care of us. It gives us air, water, and food."

"So why can't we take as much as we want?"

ERIC, I'M SERIOUS.

"Because one day it could all run out."

"Well, as long as I get mine, I don't care," sneered Eric.

CHAPTER 8
THRASH THE TRASH

I follow the trail of litter down the hall. I'm picking up the last gum wrapper when out of the boys' bathroom jumps my archenemy, Trashman, with a trail of toilet paper stuck to his shoe.

"Curses!" exclaims Trashman when he sees the clean floor. He takes off down the hall, the toilet paper fluttering behind him.

"Bummer!" I say and in a flash I become:

Earthman!—protector of the environment and more.

I take off after Trashman, who is knocking over garbage cans out in the school yard. When he sees me he starts throwing garbage.

I pick up a garbage-can lid and use it as a shield.

"Curses," says Trashman. He hurls a banana peel at me.

I pick him up, dump him into a trash can, and close the lid.

CHAPTER 9
EXHAUSTED

After school I decide to go to the market.

"Hubie, where are you going?"

"To the store, Mom."

"Let me drive you."

"Thanks, Mom, I'll just ride my bike."

"I could drive you—it would be a lot easier."

"Yeah, but Mom, it wouldn't be better for our planet."

"Hubie, it won't be too bad."

"But Mom, each little bit adds up to a BIG lot!"

A BICYCLE RIDER IS CALLED A CYCLIST.

PASSING BELL

LIGHT

OFF-ROAD TIRES

LEATHER SADDLE

AIR BOOSTER

HIGH-SPEED SPROCKET AND CHAIN

MASTER MECHANIC

"Hey, I need to do some shopping, too."

"Great! We can go together."

"On your bike?"

"No, Mom, we can walk together and talk and take Tailspin with us. It will be nice."

CHAPTER 10
ALL WRAPPED UP

We walk and talk on the way to the store.

Tailspin gets to sniff every fire hydrant along the way.

When we arrive at the market Mom asks, "Do you want to help me shop?"

"Sure, Mom."

"I need a package of tomatoes, a package of carrots, and a package of grapes. Will you get them?"

"No, Mom."

"No?"

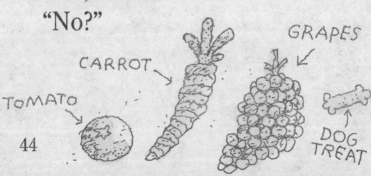

TOMATO

CARROT

GRAPES

DOG TREAT

44

SKULL → HELLO.

"Mom, I'll get the tomatoes, carrots, and grapes, but without the packaging. It's just extra trash we don't need and we'll just throw it away."

THESE LOOK GOOD.

NO, MOM.

While I'm picking fresh tomatoes, Trashman jumps out from behind the onions and wraps me up in plastic.

I can't move. But I can say "Bummer!"

Suddenly, there's a flash of lightning, a clap of thunder, and ta-da! Earthman appears.

I spin out of the plastic, pick up Trashman, bag him, and dump him in the recycling bin.

CHAPTER 11
THE GRASS IS ALWAYS GREENER

When I get home that night I watch some television. The news anchor says, "Next year they're preparing a manned mission to Mars to see if it is a habitable planet. It will cost 100 billion dollars."

"Mom, what does 'habitable' mean?"

"Well, Hubie, it means that people can live there."

"But Mom, we *have* a habitable planet."

"Unfortunately, Hubie, at the rate people are polluting the rivers, poisoning the oceans, and making the air unbreathable . . . it may not be for long."

49

"In other words, Mom, we have a habitable planet, but we're ruining it . . . so we're looking for another one."

"That's about it, Hubie."

"Why don't we just fix the one we have?"

"We're trying, Hubie, but it would be very expensive."

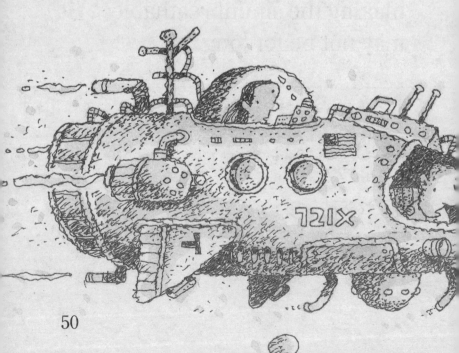

"But Mom, it's also very expensive to find another planet."

"And everyone in the world would have to work together to make it happen."

"We work together at school."

"I know, Hubie. And when you work together you can accomplish anything."

SOLO, WHAT DID YOU FIND?

IT'S A DEAD PLANET, CAPTAIN.

CHAPTER 12

THE BATTLE FOR EARTH

As everyone sleeps, thousands of giant garbage cans from space enter into our atmosphere. They carry an army, a navy, and an air force of polluters. They circle the globe and land in the water and cover the planet. Who can stop them?

Who can save Earth . . . ? Who but Earthman!

"Bummer!"

There's a flash of lightning, a clap of thunder, a drum roll, and Earthman is up and out the window into the night sky.

One by one I confront the polluters and hurl them back out into space. I battle them all night, but there are too many of them. There are tens of thousands— they are everywhere.

SWEAT ⟶

I wake up. I am sweating. Even
I can't save the world by myself!
It's going to take *everyone*!

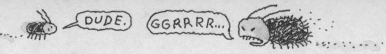

CHAPTER 13
WHAT YOU CAN DO

There are many things you can do to help Earthman. Here are just a few:

• Recycle all of your plastic, metal, glass, and paper items.

• Find new uses for old items around the house.

• Bring reusable bags to the store instead of getting plastic bags for your groceries.

MOM, WE CAN USE YOUR OLD IRON FOR A DOORSTOP.

AND WE CAN GRIND UP THIS BONE TO MAKE CHALK.

- Turn off lights when not in a room.
- Don't waste water when brushing your teeth.
- Start a vegetable garden at school or home.
- Walk, bike, and carpool whenever you can.
- Power down and unplug electronic devices.

← CARPOOL

- Plant a tree.
- Take a shorter shower.
- Don't be a litterbug. Pick up trash even if it's not yours.
- Shop at the local farmers' market.
- Turn down the thermostat.
- Buy products with less packaging.

CHAPTER 14
YES, WE CAN!

I get all of my friends to help.

"If we each pitch in, together we can save our planet and keep it habitable," I tell them.

"After school we could all go out and pick up a piece of trash," says Penny.

"Then we could collect empty bottles and cans and return them to the market," says Derek.

"We'll be rich!" says Eric.

"And after that we could plant a garden," says Freddy.

"And I'll just take a shower once a year," says Eric.

"Then you'd be polluting the atmosphere," laughs Doris.

"Let's start now," I say. "Then we'll all be superheroes."

And we were!

OLD
SODA
CAN
↘

CHAPTER 15
ECOLOGY RIDDLES

Learning to take care of the environment is fun. Here are some riddles which are also fun!

When is Earth sad?
When it's down in the dumps.

What one habit does every creature on Earth share?
Our habitat.

When is a boat cheapest to buy?
When it's on sail.

"Knock, knock."
"Who's there?"
"Trash can."
"Trash can who?"
"Trash can ruin the world."

What do you call it when the air
is filled with pigs?
Sma-hog.

What do you call it when the air
is filled with rabbits?
Hare pollution.

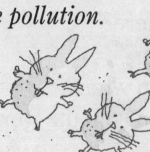

What race is everyone in?
The human race.